STORIES THAT NEVER GROW OLD

BEST LOVED STORIES RETOLD BY WATTY PIPER

Illustrated by
George and Doris Hauman

PLATT & MUNK, *Publishers*

A Division of Grosset & Dunlap

NEW YORK

CONT

1982 PRINTING
Copyright © MCMXXXVIII and MCMLXIX
The Platt & Munk Co., Inc., Bronx, N.Y. 10472
All rights reserved. Made in the United States of America.
ISBN 0-448-42004-X
Library of Congress Catalog Card Number: 59-14646

ENTS

THE UGLY DUCKLING

Mother Duck once built her nest beside the wall of a great castle. There was a moat around the wall. It was filled with water in which many ducks and geese swam.

Mother Duck found it very lonesome sitting on her eggs day after day. She did not have many visitors. Her friends liked better to swim about in the moat, than to sit and chat with her.

However, she knew that she must not let her eggs grow cold, so she sat on them patiently, day after day. One morning she heard a crack, and a tiny yellow duck pushed its way out of the egg. Soon there was another crack—and another—and another—until every egg except one had broken. This last egg was larger than the others.

As Mother Duck was wondering why it did not crack, old Grandmother Duck, who was swimming by, waddled ashore.

"How are you?" she quacked.

"Very well, thank you," Mother Duck replied. "All my eggs have hatched except one. Come in and see my pretty ducklings."

"What fine ducklings," the old Grandmother said. "But why waste your time sitting on that large egg any longer? I'm sure it's a turkey's egg, and a little turkey is a great bother to a duck. I know because I hatched one long ago. He was so afraid of the water that he wouldn't even wet his toes."

"I may as well sit on it a little longer," said Mother Duck, "I've sat so long now, that I'd like to finish the hatching."

"Do as you like," said the old Grandmother Duck, waddling back to the moat. "But remember that I warned you!"

The next day the large egg cracked and out came the strangest looking duck she had ever seen. Instead of being yellow and fluffy, like the other ducklings, it was an ugly greenish gray color and it had a long neck and long, awkward legs.

"He's the ugliest child I ever had," thought Mother Duck. But she treated him kindly and tried not to let him feel that he was different from the others.

Soon she decided that it was time to teach her little ones to swim. She led the way under the leaves and waddled ahead of them to the moat.

"Quack! Quack!" she called. "Follow me into the water and use your feet as I use mine."

The ducklings waddled into the water and spread their little webbed feet. In a few minutes they were swimming as well as Mother Duck herself.

"My Ugly Duckling swims as well as the others," thought Mother Duck, "so Grandmother Duck was wrong when she said he would be a turkey."

"Now we're going to the poultry yard," she called. She led the way out of the water and the little ones followed. A few minutes later they waddled into the poultry yard, where there were many other ducks, as well as geese and hens and turkeys. Such a quacking and clucking and gobbling you never heard!

Everyone stared at the Ugly Duckling, and a young drake laughed out loud.

"Did anyone ever see such a ridiculous looking bird?" he said. With his sharp bill he pecked at the poor little Ugly Duckling.

"Stop!" said Mother Duck. "I will not have my duckling ill-treated." The young drake went away, but the largest turkey in the yard came up and looked at the frightened little bird.

"Gobble! Gobble! Gobble!" he said, "Who ever brought this ugly duckling into our yard?"

"Keep away," Mother Duck said. "I will not allow anyone to torment him."

But Mother Duck could not be beside the Ugly Duckling all the time, and whenever she was away from him for a moment, someone teased him or pecked at him. The Ugly Duckling was given no peace. Even his own brothers and sisters made fun of him, and the girl who came out to feed them kicked him away.

Day after day things grew worse. The Ugly Duckling was treated so badly, that he decided to run away. He ran toward

the fence, spreading his wings, and by using all his strength he managed to fly over it. The little birds in the bushes where he landed flew away in fright. "That is because I am so ugly that I terrify them," he thought sadly.

He traveled on until he reached a great marsh where crowds of wild ducks were swimming. The Ugly Duckling swam out among them, bowing politely this way and that, as Mother Duck had taught him to do. The wild ducks made fun of him, but they did not peck him as the birds in the poultry yard had done.

"You're very ugly," one of them told him, "we don't mind having you around but don't try to marry into any of our families."

The poor little duck had no thought of marriage. All he wanted was a chance to find food and a comfortable place to sleep. He swam around the marsh and found plenty to eat and spent the night under some tall rushes at the edge of the water.

Before long the wild ducks spread their wings and flew away.

The Ugly Duckling was left alone in the marsh. The days grew colder, and food was harder and harder to find. At length the water began to freeze and the place where he swam became smaller and smaller. One morning he was frozen in and could not move. He thought the end of his life had come, but a peasant who was passing, broke the ice with his wooden shoe and carried the half frozen little duck home. Here he soon thawed out in the heat of the cottage.

The peasant had two children who wanted to play with the little bird, but the Ugly Duckling was afraid of them and flew wildly about. He flopped into the milk pan, and when the peasant's wife shouted at him he flew from the milk into the butter crock and then into the flour barrel. But this time he was no longer gray but white with flour. The poor woman ran at him with the fire tongs, but fortunately the door was open and the Ugly Duckling managed to escape.

The rest of the winter was a time of great suffering for him. He almost starved, and the only shelter he could find was a clump of dried rushes. But he lived through the cold months and when the spring came, the sun began to warm the marsh and the plants began to grow. Soon the Ugly Duckling felt warm and comfortable.

The song birds that had flown south for the winter began to come back. As the Ugly Duckling heard their songs he felt a desire to fly. He spread his wings and rose from the ground. His wings had grown long and strong and they made a rushing sound as he flew into the air.

How beautiful the world looked! Apple trees were in bloom and little streams rippled through green fields. The Ugly Duckling flew on and on, enjoying the warm sun and the blue sky and the lovely places over which he passed. After a while he saw a great house with a beautiful garden. In the garden was a pond that looked like a sheet of clear glass.

The Ugly Duckling swooped down and lighted on the pond. "How I should love to live here," he thought. Just then he saw three wonderful birds come out of the bushes and walk down to the water. They had gleaming white plumage and long graceful necks.

"They must be swans, the royal birds," the Ugly Duckling thought. He felt sad as he looked at them. "This pond of course belongs to them, and they will not allow me to stay," he thought. He was about to spread his wings and fly away, but a great sadness came over him.

As the three swans swam toward him, he bowed his head. But as he looked at his reflection in the clear water, he saw that he was no longer gray and ugly. His neck was long and graceful and his plumage was glistening white, like that of the three swans. When they came close to him they did not peck at him or make fun of him. They stroked him gently with their bills and welcomed him to the pond.

Just then two children ran out of the house, bringing bread for the swans.

"There's a new one," called the little boy.

"Yes, and how beautiful he is," the little girl replied, "more beautiful than any of the others."

When they heard the words, the three swans bowed their graceful necks in honor of their new comrade.

How happy he was! After so much suffering to have everything so comfortable and pleasant! After having everyone make fun of him and torment him, to be welcomed by the most beautiful birds in the world! He shook his white plumes and said joyfully:

"It does not matter that one was hatched in a duck's nest, if one came from a swan's egg. I never dreamed that such happiness was in store for me, in the days when I was called the Ugly Duckling."

THE BREMEN TOWN MUSICIANS

A farmer lived near the town of Bremen. He had a donkey who had been a hard working animal, but now was growing weak with age. One day the old donkey was eating grass near the farm house.

"Old Hee-Haw is getting old," he heard the farmer say to his wife. "Tomorrow I'll take him to market and sell him to the tanner. With what he gives me for the skin, and a little more, I can buy a young donkey."

Poor old Hee-Haw began to shiver and shake. But suddenly he threw up his head. "Why should I be sold to the tanner?" he said to himself. "Age hasn't harmed my fine voice. In Bremen Town the people love music. I'll go there and earn my living as a musician."

Feeling much better, the old donkey trotted down the road to Bremen Town. After a while he stopped for a few bites of grass beside the road. Lying in the grass was a dog panting very hard.

"Why do you pant so, friend?" asked Hee-Haw. "And what is your name?"

"My name is Bruno," replied the dog. "For years I've guarded my master's house and his flocks, but now I'm old and my sight is

17

not sharp enough for him. I overheard him telling his wife that he was going to knock me on the head and get a younger dog. So I ran away. But now I don't know where to go or how to earn my living."

"Can you still bark?" asked the donkey.

"Oh, yes," the dog replied. "Bow-wow-wow!"

"You have a fine deep note," said Hee-Haw. "Join me and go to Bremen Town. There we can make our living as musicians."

Up jumped the old dog, and side by side the two animals trotted toward Bremen town. A little farther along they came to a place where a cat was sitting in the middle of the road, looking very sad.

What is troubling you, mistress cat?" asked Hee-Haw.

"I'm homeless and hungry," said the cat. "For years I caught mice in my mistress's house; but now I can't move quickly enough, and the mice escape. I heard my mistress planning to tie a stone to my neck and drop me into the river. So I ran away. But now I don't know how to find a bite to eat."

"Can you still meow?" asked the donkey.

"Oh, yes indeed," replied the cat. "Me-ow!"

"That's a very sweet tone," said the donkey, " and should make excellent harmony with my bray and Bruno's bark. We are going

to Bremen Town to earn our living as musicians. Won't you come with us."

"Thank you," said the cat. "My name is Felix and I shall be glad to meow with you."

Soon they passed a farmyard where a rooster was perched on top of the barn.

"Cock-a-doodle-do!" he crowed, flapping his wings.

"Why do you crow so loudly?" called the donkey.

"Because tomorrow will be a fine day," replied the rooster. "I always crow extra loud and long for fine weather. But it annoys my mistress. I just heard her tell the maid that she would wring my neck tomorrow and make soup of me."

"Then why not come with us?" suggested the donkey. "We are bound for Bremen Town to make our living as musicians."

"I'll go with pleasure," said the rooster. "My name is Chanticleer."

So they all went on toward Bremen Town.

Soon it began to grow dark and the donkey said they would have to spend the night in the woods. He and Bruno lay down under a tree. Felix climbed to one of the lower branches, and Chanticleer flew to the very top.

"There must be a house in the forest," he called down. "I see a light through the leaves."

"In that case," said Hee-Haw, getting up, "perhaps we can find more comfortable quarters than this rough ground. Where there's a house there's usually a barn."

They set off through the forest and in a few minutes came to the house.

"I'm the tallest," said Hee-Haw. "I'll go softly to the window and see what's inside."

He walked to the window and looked into the room. Then he walked back to the place where his friends were standing.

"I saw four robbers," he brayed, very softly. "On the table were piles of gold and jewels, and there were all sorts of good things to eat and drink."

"That would be a fine place for us to spend the night," growled Bruno, "if only we could get rid of the robbers."

"Robbers are easily frightened," purred Felix, "because they are not honorable."

"So they are," crowed Chanticleer, in a very small voice. "If, all together, we make as much noise as we can, perhaps we could frighten them away."

They all crept up to the window. Hee-Haw stood with his chin just above the sill. Bruno jumped on his back. Felix jumped on Bruno's back and Chanticleer flew up and perched on Felix's back.

"Now when I nod my head," said Hee-Haw, "let us, each one, make as much noise as possible."

Then, as Hee-Haw nodded: The Donkey brayed, the Dog barked, the Cat meowed and the Rooster crowed and flapped his wings.

"What in the world is that?" shouted one of the robbers, and all four sprang up from the table in great fear.

With a whir of his wings, Chanticleer flew in and put out the light. Felix came after him with a hiss. Bruno followed with a growl, and old Hee-Haw jumped through the window with a loud bray and a clatter of hoofs against the window frame.

The robbers were so frightened, that they ran out of the house and didn't stop until they had put a full mile between themselves and the terrible noises that had come upon them so suddenly.

"The gold can wait," said Hee-Haw, sitting down at the table. "I'm hungry."

"So am I," said Bruno taking his place at the other end. Felix sat on one side and Chanticleer on the other side of the table, and when they got up again there was little left of the feast.

"Now," said the donkey, "I'm going to drag in a bunch of hay and lie here by the door."

"This thick rug will be my bed," said the dog.

"I'll sleep on the warm hearth," purred the cat.

"That rafter near the ceiling will make a perfect perch for me," crowed the rooster.

Meanwhile the robbers had run until they were tired out.

"What are we running away from, anyway?" asked one as they came to a stop.

"It must have been a troop of hobgoblins," said another.

"Yes, I never heard such horrible noises in all my life," said the third.

"Hobgoblins or no hobgoblins," said the fourth, "I'm going back for my gold and jewels."

The four robbers walked back through the forest. When they reached the house all was still and dark.

"I'll go in first," said the fourth robber, "and you all come close behind me."

He groped around until he found a candle.

"The fire's nearly out," he called, "but there are a few sparks that will be enough to light the candle."

He marched boldly to the fireplace, but what he took for sparks were the fiery eyes of Felix, glaring through the darkness. As he stooped, the cat sprang up with a hiss and buried her claws in his arm. The robber screamed and turned to run out of the door, but as he turned he stepped on Bruno's tail. The old dog growled and bit him in the leg. Then Chanticleer flew down and pecked his neck, and, as he came to the doorway, Hee-Haw kicked out with his hind legs and landed the robber on his back outside the door.

Terribly frightened they all ran away as fast as they could, and they never dared go back to the house again.

The four musicians settled down in comfort. With the gold and jewels the robbers had left, they were able to buy all the food they needed, so they never went to Bremen Town after all.

But once a year, they give a concert for their own pleasure. They stand by the window as they did when they frightened the robbers, and as the donkey nods his head, all together they begin:

"Hee-haw! Hee-haw!" "Bow-wow! Bow-wow!"
"Me-ow! Me-ow!" "Cock-a-doodle-doo-oo-oo-oo!"

THE FOX AND THE STORK

Reynard, the Fox, liked to play tricks on all his animal and bird friends. One day he invited Long Legs, the Stork, to dinner. When his guest arrived, Reynard led the way to the table. He had prepared a good thick soup, which he knew Long Legs liked better than anything else. But, to play a joke on the Stork, the Fox had served it in a low, flat dish.

"Eat, my friend," said Reynard, and with his long red tongue he lapped up the good soup. But poor Long Legs, with his long bill, could get only a few drops of the good soup. So he went home hungrier than when he came.

Not long afterward, he invited Master Reynard to dine with him. When the Fox reached the Stork's home, Long Legs led the way to the dinner table. Now, instead of being served in a low, flat dish, the soup was served in a tall jar.

"Eat, my friend," invited Long Legs, and put his long bill down into the delicious soup. But Reynard could not get even the tip of his nose into the small mouth of the jar. He had to be satisfied with a few drops that fell down the outside.

So he went home hungrier than when he came, but he remembered the trick he had played on the Stork and had to admit to himself that for once he had met his match.

THE BOY AND THE NORTH WIND

A long time ago, in Norway, a boy lived with his mother. One day she gave him a bowl and said, "Go to the storehouse and bring me some meal for our porridge."

The boy crossed the yard and filled the bowl in the storehouse. But the moment he came out of the door, the North Wind came with a roar and blew all the meal out of the bowl.

The boy went back into the storehouse and got some more meal, but as soon as he stepped out of the door, the Wind blew the meal away again. Once more he filled the bowl, and once more the Wind emptied it.

Then the boy was angry. He started toward the North, where the Wind had his home. He walked and walked, and it was almost night when he reached the palace of the North Wind.

"Good day," said the boy to the Wind. "Thank you for calling on me yesterday."

"Good day," the Wind replied gruffly. "There's no need of thanks. What's brought you here?"

"I came to ask you to give back the meal you blew from my bowl," said the boy. "We are very poor, and if you keep blowing our meal away, we are likely to starve."

"I have no meal," said the North Wind, "but I'll give you a tablecloth that will be better than many bushels of grain. When you want to eat, say to the cloth, "Cloth, cover the table and serve a fine meal.""

The boy thanked the North Wind and started home with the tablecloth, but darkness came upon him before he had gone far. There was an inn near by and the boy went in. He seated himself and said, "Cloth, cover the table and serve a fine meal." Immediately a delicious dinner was before him.

The other guests in the inn were wonderstruck. The innkeeper's wife determined that the tablecloth should belong to her. In the middle of the night she crept to the place where the boy was asleep and took the cloth from him. In its place she left one of her own that looked very much like it.

When he reached home, the boy told his mother all his adventures and showed her the tablecloth. "It is a magic cloth," he said, "and serves a meal whenever I tell it to."

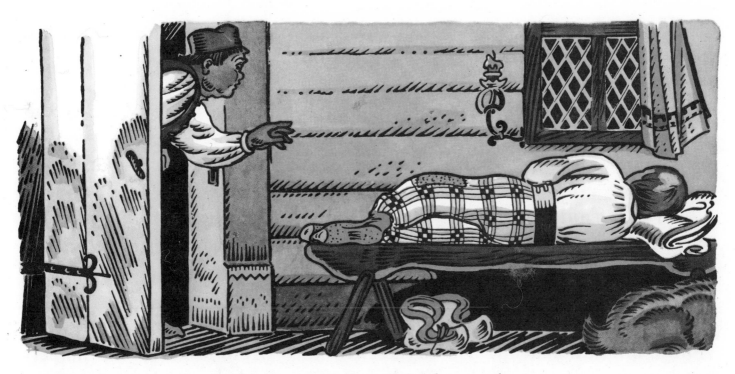

"I'll believe it when I see it," said his mother.

The boy put the cloth on the table and said, "Cloth, cover the table and serve a fine meal." But the cloth lay just as he had put it, for of course it was not the magic cloth.

"Well," said the boy, "I'll have to go back to the North Wind and tell him his tablecloth is no good." When he came to the palace of the North Wind he was feeling very angry.

"That tablecloth that you gave me is no good," he declared. "It worked once in the inn, but when I reached home it had lost its magic."

"Someone must have robbed you," replied the North Wind. "I have no more tablecloths, but here is a goat who will keep you supplied with money. When your purse is empty, say, "Goat, give me gold," and immediately it will be filled with gold coins.

The boy thanked the Wind and led the goat to the same inn where he had spent the night before. He found that his purse was empty and said, "Goat, give me gold." Immediately the purse was full of golden coins.

That night the innkeeper crept to the place where the boy was sleeping and led the goat away. In its place he left one of his own goats.

When the boy reached home, he told his mother about the goat's power to fill his purse with gold.

"I'll believe it when I see it," said his mother.

The boy gave the order, "Goat, give me gold," but of course no gold appeared. The boy was angrier than ever. Back he went to the palace of the North Wind and told him the goat would not give gold.

"Well," said the North Wind, "I have nothing left to give you except that old stick you see standing in the corner. If you say to it, 'Stick, lay on,' it will beat anyone who is bothering you. When you want it to stop, say, 'Stick, leave off.' "

This time when he came to the inn, the boy resolved that he would not fall asleep. He lay down and pretended to be asleep, but he kept himself awake. At length he heard the innkeeper creeping toward him. The innkeeper had not seen the stick do anything, but he felt sure it must have some such magic as the tablecloth and the goat had. So he resolved to steal it.

Just as he was reaching for it, the boy opened his eyes and said, "Stick, lay on."

Up jumped the stick and began to beat the innkeeper. He ran around the room, jumping over tables and chairs, but could not get away from the stick.

"Oh, dear! Oh, dear!" he cried. "Call to your stick to stop and I'll give back the tablecloth and the goat."

The boy gave the order. "Stick, leave off," and immediately it jumped into his hand and was still.

Then the innkeeper brought out the tablecloth and the goat and the boy started for home happily, swinging the stick in his hand. When he reached the cottage, he said, "Cloth, cover the table and serve a fine meal." And there before his mother's eyes was the finest dinner she had ever seen. Then he said, "Goat, give me gold," and his purse was piled with golden coins.

"We shall never have to worry about a bowlful of meal again," said the boy, "and we'll keep the stick standing in the corner, to be used if anyone tries to rob us of our tablecloth or our goat."

HANSEL AND GRETEL

Near a great forest lived a poor woodcutter with his two children, Hansel and Gretel, and their stepmother. Times were very hard, and a day came when there was no food in the cottage except a little stale bread.

That night the stepmother said to her husband: "I can't bear to see the children starve. It would be better to take them into the forest and leave them. There they might at least find some berries or roots to eat."

The woodcutter was very sad at the thought of parting from his children, but he felt that his wife knew best.

So next morning he said to Hansel and Gretel: "Come with me into the forest. While I cut wood you can look for berries."

Gretel was glad, but Hansel had overheard what his stepmother had said the night before, and knew that his father intended to leave them in the woods.

Their stepmother gave each of them a small piece of bread. "This is for your lunch," she said.

31

Gretel put her piece into her pocket. But Hansel crumbled his and every few steps along the way he dropped a crumb, to mark the path they were following.

When they reached a sunny clearing in the forest their father said: "You may stay here and hunt for berries, while I go on farther to cut wood."

All morning the children looked for berries but none were to be found. At noon they ate Gretel's bread.

As evening came on, Gretel began to grow anxious.

"I wonder why father does not come," she asked.

With sorrow, Hansel told her what he had overheard their stepmother say. Gretel began to cry, but Hansel comforted her.

"Wait until the moon rises," he said. "Then the crumbs I dropped will show us the way home."

But when the moon rose, no crumbs were to be seen. The hungry birds had eaten them all. Sad and hungry, the children lay down at the foot of a tree and fell asleep.

In the morning they were awakened by the song of a beautiful bird. Looking up into the tree, they saw a bird with gleaming white feathers, singing with all his might. The bird flew to the next

tree. He seemed to be calling them. They followed, but as soon as they came beneath the tree in which he was perched, he flew on farther.

They forgot their sadness and their hunger. All day they followed the bird. Toward evening they came to an opening in the forest. Before them was a little cottage gleaming in the rays of the setting sun.

"Look, Gretel!" exclaimed Hansel, "I believe that cottage is made of gingerbread!"

"It really is," replied Gretel, running up and tasting a little piece that she had pulled from the wall. "And the roof looks as though it were shingled with butterscotch."

"The windowsills are made of chocolate," declared Hansel, breaking off a bit and eating it.

"And the windowpanes are made of clear candy," said Gretel.

At that moment the door of the cottage was opened and an old woman came out.

"What a sweet little boy and girl," she said, in a soft, wheedling voice. "Are you hungry? Come inside and I'll give you something to eat."

The children felt afraid, but they followed the old woman into the house. She gave them milk and bread and nuts and apples and pancakes and honey. When they had eaten all they could, she pointed to two little beds.

"Now go to bed, children," she said. "Sleep well, little dears!"

In a very few minutes Hansel was fast asleep. The old woman seemed kind, but Gretel did not trust her and decided to stay awake.

The old woman had only pretended to be kind; she was really a witch, who had built the house made of candy, to lure children there.

After a little time, the old witch came tiptoeing toward Gretel's bed. Gretel pretended to be asleep and the witch went to the bed where Hansel was sleeping. Gretel opened her eyes. She saw the old witch lift Hansel from his bed and carry him out of the door. All night the little girl lay wondering what had happened to her brother.

When morning came the witch shouted at Gretel to get up and gave her a pail to bring water from the pump.

Gretel ran out to fill the pail and was astonished to see Hansel lying asleep in a huge cage. She ran over to the cage and called her brother. When he opened his eyes he was bewildered.

"How did I ever come here?" he asked, looking around at the bars of the cage. Gretel told him how she had seen the old witch carry him from his bed. Hansel began to shake the door of the cage, but Gretel told him that the witch had no doubt locked it by the magic power of her wand and that only the same magic power could open it. Just then she heard the angry voice of the witch calling to her to hurry. She filled the pail at the pump and ran back into the cottage.

All day the witch kept her busy, sweeping and scrubbing and doing all sorts of hard tasks. Late in the afternoon she ordered Gretel to chop wood.

"We must heat the oven," said the old witch, chuckling with wicked glee.

Gretel wondered why the witch wanted the oven heated, for there was no bread ready to be baked. But she kept on chopping and the witch kept putting wood into the fireplace until there was a great big blaze. Then the witch opened the iron door of the big baking oven and peered in.

"Crawl into the oven, girl," she ordered, "and see if it's hot enough."

Now, indeed, Gretel was frightened, for she knew that the witch intended to shut her up in the hot oven. She would have tried to run away, but she could not leave Hansel a prisoner in the cage outside. She must think up some way to free him.

"I'm afraid I can't get in," she said. "The opening is too small."

"Silly goose!" snapped the old witch. "It's plenty big enough for a little girl. See, I could even get into it myself."

Stooping down, she put her head and shoulders into the oven. This was just the chance for which Gretel had been waiting. She grasped the iron door with both hands and slammed it against the old witch, pushing her clear into the oven. Then she closed the door and fastened it.

The witch was furious. She shrieked and banged on the door, but Gretel knew that she could not get out, for she had left her magic wand lying on the table.

Picking up the wand, Gretel ran to the cage where Hansel was imprisoned. With one touch of the magic wand she opened the cage door and Hansel sprang out.

The white bird who had led the children to the witch's cottage flew down from a tree. As he touched the ground he became a handsome young Prince, and the cage, in which Hansel had been held prisoner, melted away into thin air. In the place where it had been, the children saw a pile of gold pieces and precious stones.

The Prince bowed to Gretel. "I have waited many years for this release from my enchantment," he said. "The old witch stole me from my father's castle when I was only a child. The spell she put upon me could never be broken until she was outwitted by a mortal. You are the first mortal who has been able to outwit her," he said, bowing to Gretel again.

"The witch took those jewels and gold pieces when she stole me," he said. "I beg that you will accept them as a token of my gratitude. When I am safe again in my father's castle, I should like to have you visit me. Good-bye," he said and he turned and walked into the forest and was lost to sight among the trees.

Hansel and Gretel filled their pockets with gold and precious stones. Then they set out, hoping they might meet someone who could tell them how to reach their home. They had not gone far when they saw their father and stepmother coming toward them.

"Dear children," exclaimed the stepmother, "we could not bear to think of you alone in the forest. If we must starve, we'll all starve together."

"But we need not starve," said Gretel and Hansel, holding out their hands filled with gold and jewels.

So they all went home and lived happily ever after, and there was never any poverty in the woodcutter's cottage again.

THE BOY WHO CRIED "WOLF"!

Many years ago in a beautiful valley in Greece, a poor farmer had built his house. His most valued possession was a flock of sheep. They gave wool for clothing and meat for the table, and the farmer guarded them carefully day and night.

Often he took his young son to the pasture where the sheep grazed. The boy loved to go with his father. He liked to play with the lambs and to eat bread and cheese under a tree at noontime. When he was thirsty he drank from a stream that ran through the meadows. One day his father taught him to carve a pipe from a willow twig, and to play little tunes on it.

Years went by, and one day the farmer said to his son: "You are old enough to guard the sheep now, and there is other work about the farm that I should do. Go with them to the pasture and guard them as I have taught you to do."

At first the young shepherd enjoyed taking care of the flock. He kept the lambs from straying and found new meadows when the sheep had eaten all the grass in the field. To amuse himself he made up new tunes to play on his pipe.

But after a while he began to find the work tiresome. "Here

I am," he grumbled to himself, "with only a lot of stupid animals for company. I'd like to hear the sound of a human voice once in a while, but all that I hear is the silly bleating of a flock of sheep —'Ba-a-a! Ba-a-a! Ba-a-a!'"

He complained to his father. "I'm tired of spending all my time with a flock of stupid sheep."

"I'm sorry, son," the father replied, "but there is no one else to send. For many years I have watched the flock, but now there is other work that needs to be done. In a few years your brother will be old enough to act as shepherd. For the present, there is no one except you whom I can trust to guard the sheep."

The boy felt ashamed. He knew how hard his father had worked to give his family a comfortable home and enough to eat. So he tried hard to take an interest in the sheep and for a time he was content. Then he began to feel sorry for himself again.

"No one ever led such a stupid life as mine," he thought. "I wish a wolf would come from the forest. That at least would give me a little excitement."

Then an idea came into his head.

"The people in the village can hear me if I shout," he said to himself, and raising his voice he shouted "Help! Help! Wolf! Wolf!"

The villagers came running with spears and pitchforks, but when they reached the pasture, of course there was no wolf. The boy told them that the wolf had run back into the forest. Some of the men doubted him, but a few felt sorry for the boy and stayed with him for the rest of the day.

A few days later he decided to try the same trick again.

"Help! Help! Wolf! Wolf!" he shouted, and again the villagers came to his aid.

This time, however, the few who had been so friendly before, were suspicious when they found that there was no wolf.

"If there had been a wolf here," said the Mayor of the village, "there would be some tracks of his paws, in the soft earth beside the stream."

The boy pointed out some tracks, but the Mayor said they had been made by sheep, not by a wolf.

No one stayed with the young shepherd this time, and as they went back to their work the villagers were very angry.

"I believe that boy was deceiving us," one said.

"I'm sure of it," another agreed.

"If he calls again," said the Mayor, "let us pay no attention to him."

A few days later a wolf really did come from the forest and dashed into the middle of the flock.

"Help! Help! Wolf! Wolf!" the young shepherd shouted in terror, for he had nothing but a shepherd's crook as a weapon, and he knew he could not overcome a huge, fierce wolf with that.

The villagers paid no attention to his cries but went on with their work. The boy started to run toward them, shouting all the way. When he came to the village, he found the Mayor standing in the doorway of his house.

"Why did you not come when I shouted?" the boy demanded. "A great hungry wolf came and killed several of my lambs."

"I'm sorry to hear that," the Mayor replied, "but you have deceived us twice and we thought you were deceiving us again. If you want people to help you when you are in trouble, you must call for help only when you really need it. No one believes a liar, even when he speaks the truth."

BILLY GOAT GRUFF

Once there were three billy goats who lived in a valley. They were nearly always hungry, because they had eaten up all the good grass.

"Let us go up into the hills," said the smallest. "I have heard that the grass there is long and thick and juicy."

"A good idea," agreed the middle-sized goat. "We need to get some fat on our bones before winter comes."

"You two go ahead," said Billy Goat Gruff, who was the largest of the three. "There is just a little patch of grass here that I want to finish off. Then I will come."

To reach the hills, the billy goats had to cross a bridge over a roaring torrent. An ugly troll made his home under the bridge. His nose was so long that it stuck out a foot before his face and he had great big red eyes.

The smallest billy goat walked daintily uphill and started across the bridge.

"Trip-a-ty trip! Trip-a-ty trip!" clicked his little hoofs on the planks.

"Who is crossing my bridge?" roared the troll, poking his ugly long nose up over the edge.

"I am the smallest of the billy goats," said the little goat.

"I am coming up to catch you," screamed the troll. "I don't allow billy goats on my bridge. You will make a good supper for me."

"Oh, please don't catch me," begged the little goat. "I am so thin I would hardly make a mouthful for you. Wait for my brother who is just behind. He is much bigger than I am."

"Very well. Be off with you," shouted the troll. And the smallest of the billy goats scampered across the bridge and up into the hills.

In a little while the middle-sized billy goat came to the bridge.

"Trap-a-ty trap! Trap-a-ty trap!" clapped his hoofs on the planks.

"Who's that crossing my bridge?" shouted the troll, poking up his ugly long nose.

"I am the middle-sized billy goat," replied the goat. "I am going up into the hills to get fat."

"Oh, no, you are not!" roared the troll. "You are going to make a good supper for me! I'm coming up to catch you now."

"Please don't catch me," begged the middle-sized goat. "Wait for my brother, Billy Goat Gruff. He's much bigger than I am."

"Very well," grumbled the troll. "But don't come back over my bridge again."

The middle-sized goat scampered across and was soon in the hills with his little brother.

Pretty soon Billy Goat Gruff came along and started across the bridge.

"Trop-a-ty trop. Trop-a-ty trop!" clopped his feet on the planks.

"Who's that crossing my bridge?" shouted the troll, poking up his ugly long nose.

"I'm Billy Goat Gruff," shouted the largest of the goats, "and it isn't your bridge."

"Yes it is," shouted the troll louder than ever, "and I don't allow billy goats to cross it. I'm coming up to catch you. You'll make a fine supper for me."

He scrambled up on the bridge and made a rush at Billy Goat Gruff. But he had forgotten the sharp horns that billy goats carry on their heads.

"Two can play at this game," shouted Billy Goat Gruff, and

with his sharp horns he rushed at the troll so fiercely that he butt-
ed him right off the bridge onto the rocks below.

"A bridge belongs to anyone who wants to cross it," he called
down. "No troll can stop Billy Goat Gruff."

Soon he was with his brothers, eating the thick, juicy grass at
the top of the hill.

"We have plenty of fat to keep us warm through the winter,"
said the middle-sized goat a few weeks later. "It is time we were
going down to the valley again."

"I hope the troll isn't under the bridge," said the smallest of
the goats, beginning to tremble.

"If he is," said Billy Goat Gruff, "I'll butt him off onto the rocks
again."

But when they came to the bridge there was no sign of
any troll and one by one they crossed into the valley.

"Trip-a-ty trip!" "Trap-a-ty trap!" "Trop-a-ty trop" went their
hoofs on the planks.

"No troll who ever lived could keep me from crossing a bridge,"
said Billy Goat Gruff.

Soon the smallest billy goat, the middle-sized billy goat and
Billy Goat Gruff were home in the nice shed Farmer Brown had
built for them, to spend the nights during the winter.

THE PIED PIPER OF HAMELIN

Many, many years ago, in the city of Hamelin, the people were having a dreadful time. Every house in the town was full of rats. Large rats, small rats, old rats, young rats—they were everywhere! They fought with the dogs and killed the cats. They hid under beds and danced on chairs. They jumped on tables and took the food from the plates. And at night they made such a shrieking and a squeaking that nobody could get a wink of sleep.

The people became very angry because the Mayor could not get rid of these pests. They went to the town hall, where he was sitting with his Counsellors.

"What are you going to do about these rats?" they asked.

"What *can* I do?" the Mayor replied. "We have tried everything that has ever been heard of, but nothing seems to have any effect."

"Better try again, Mr. Mayor," warned the citizens, "or we'll find a mayor who can do something."

"Dear me!" exclaimed the Mayor to his Counsellors, after the angry citizens had left. "My nerves are all unstrung trying to find a way of getting rid of the rats."

As he finished speaking, there was a knock at the door.

Tap, tap, tap.

The Mayor jumped. "Dear me!" he said. "What's that? Anything that sounds like a rat makes my heart jump."

The knock came again. Tap, tap, tap.

"Come in," called the Mayor. And in came the strangest looking man anyone in the room had ever seen.

He was tall and thin. He had sharp blue eyes and light hair, but very dark skin. One half of his long cloak was yellow and the other half red. As he walked over to the table where the Mayor and his counsellors were sitting, they saw that he was smiling and that his fingers were playing with a pipe, that hung from a red and yellow scarf, which he wore around his neck.

"Please your Honors," he said, "I am known as the Pied Piper. I have a charm by which I can make any living creature follow me. If I rid your city of the rats which plague you, will you pay me a thousand guilders?"

"A thousand guilders? We'll gladly pay fifty thousand," said the Mayor.

"All I want is a thousand guilders," the Piper replied.

"Agreed," said the Mayor.

Then the Pied Piper stepped into the street and raised his pipe to his lips. For a moment he stood there smiling. Then he began to play, walking slowly down the street toward the river.

He had not blown more than three musical notes when there was a squeaking and a rumbling as the rats came tumbling from every house. Large rats and small rats, thin rats and fat rats, old rats and young rats, brown rats, gray rats and black rats, they ran—pushing and squealing and dancing behind the Pied Piper.

He went slowly along the street, and at every corner, fresh crowds of rats joined the procession. The music he played was a magic call that made them forget everything else, and when he came to the river bank, they dashed by him into the water and disappeared.

When the people of Hamelin saw the last rat's tail sink beneath the waves, they gathered in the market place and shouted and cheered and rang the church bells joyously. The Pied Piper approached the Mayor and said, "I have rid your city of every rat. Please pay me my thousand guilders."

"A thousand guilders!" the Mayor exclaimed. "That's an outrageous sum for piping a little tune. I'll give you fifty. That pays you well for your work."

The blue eyes of the Piper gleamed. "You promised a thousand," he said. "I'm in a hurry, so don't delay me. If you make me angry, you will regret it."

The Mayor's face grew red with rage.

"Is that the way you speak to the Mayor of Hamelin?" he sputtered. "I'll give you fifty guilders. Take it and be off—or go without any pay. You'll get no thousand guilders from us."

The angry Piper stepped back into the middle of the street. Again he lifted his pipe to his lips. Before he had blown three soft notes, the people of Hamelin heard the sound of children's feet coming from all directions. Little girls and little boys, they danced and skipped and clapped their hands in joy as they followed the Pied Piper and his magic music.

The Mayor and his Counsellors were struck dumb with surprise, and all the fathers and mothers stood as though they were turned to stone. Down the street toward the river the Piper went, and the children followed.

Was he going to drown them as he had drowned the rats? Everyone watched breathless.

But when he came to the river bank he turned to the west and went toward a mountain that stood near the town.

"Ah, now they are safe," said the fathers and mothers. "When he comes to that high mountain he will have to stop. Then the children will come home again."

Just before the Pied Piper reached the mountain, a magic door opened in its side. The people of the city saw him walk through the doorway, and the happy children danced after him—all except one little lame boy, who could not keep up with the procession. As the children passed through the opening, the door closed behind them, and the mountain was just as it had always been.

The fathers and mothers ran to the little lame boy to find out what the Piper's music had said to the children. He was very sad at being left behind.

"The Piper promised us such lovely sights that everyone was glad to follow him," he told them. "The music said that he was leading us to a joyous land, where there are fruits and flowers, more wonderful than anyone in this world has ever seen. The sparrows in that country are brighter than the peacocks here, and everyone is happy and well. And just as I thought that I should go there and be cured of my lameness, the door closed and I was left outside."

Wherever it was—that wonderful land—no one in Hamelin ever learned. Years afterward, travelers told of a country called Transylvania, where there were men and women who were not like the Transylvanians. It was said that these strangers had come up out of the earth, so perhaps they were the children whom the Pied Piper had led from Hamelin. All that we know is that they never returned to their homes and the little lame boy never forgot the wonderful things the music of the Pied Piper had promised.

THE MARRIAGE OF ROBIN REDBREAST AND THE WREN

Old Brown Pussycat went for a walk beside the river. There she saw Young Robin Redbreast hopping on a brier bush.

"I'm going away! I'm going away!" he sang, as he hopped.

"Where are you going, Young Robin Redbreast?" asked Old Brown Pussycat.

"I'm going to the King's palace," replied Robin Redbreast, "to sing him a song this joyous spring morning."

"Oh, don't fly so far away from your brier," said Old Brown Pussycat. "Fly down here and I'll show you a bonny white ring around my neck."

"No, no, Old Brown Pussycat," sang Robin Redbreast. "You may catch the wee mousie, but you'll not catch me."

With these words Young Robin Redbreast flew away from the brier bush. He spread his wings and rose high above the trees. Then he flew toward the north, where he knew the King had his palace.

Soon he came to a stone wall that ran around a field. On the wall Greedy Hawk was sitting.

"Where are you going, Young Robin?" called Greedy Hawk.

"I'm going to the King's palace to sing him a song this joyous spring morning," Young Robin Redbreast sang, as he flew over Greedy Hawk.

"Come back, dear Little Robin," called Greedy Hawk, "and I'll show you a bonny feather in my wing."

But Young Robin replied: "No, no, Greedy Hawk. No, no! You may catch the little linnet, but you'll not catch me."

He flew on till he came to a high cliff. There Reynard the Fox was sitting on a flat rock.

"Where are you going, Young Robin?" Reynard called.

"I'm going to the King's palace to sing him a song this joyous spring morning," Young Robin replied.

"Come here, Young Robin," Sly Reynard coaxed. "I'll show you an interesting spot on my tail."

But Young Robin Redbreast said again: "No, no. You may deceive the little lamb, Sly Reynard, but you'll not deceive me."

He flew on till he came to the edge of a meadow where a rippling brook flowed. On the bank of the stream a Little Boy was sitting.

"Where are you going, Young Robin Redbreast?" the boy called.

"I'm going to the King's palace to sing him a song this joyous spring morning," the Robin replied.

"Don't fly so far," said the boy. "Come down and sing your song to me and I'll give you some crumbs from my bag of lunch."

But Robin Redbreast sang, as he went on his way: "No, no, Little Boy, No, no! I must hurry along or I'll be late in reaching the King's palace."

So he flew on and on until he came to the King's Palace. The King and the Queen were sitting beside a window, looking out at their fair country.

Robin Redbreast flew to the windowsill. He hopped along to one end and looked in at the Queen. She was very beautiful and she wore a golden crown with three rubies in it.

"Good morning, Your Majesty," chirped Young Robin Redbreast.

"Good morning, Robin Redbreast," replied the Queen.

Robin Redbreast hopped to the other end of the sill and looked in at the King.

"Good morning, Your Majesty," he chirped again.

"Good morning, Young Robin Redbreast," the King replied. "What brings you to my windowsill so early in the morning?"

"I've come to sing you a song this joyous spring day," said Young Robin. Then he hopped to the middle of the windowsill and sang his joyous song.

When he had finished the King said to the Queen, "I have never heard a more joyous song, have you?"

"No," the Queen replied. "It fills my heart with happiness."

"What shall we give Young Robin Redbreast for his song?" the King asked.

"Let us give him our Little Jenny Wren for his wife," suggested the Queen.

When Robin Redbreast heard the Queen's words he opened his throat and sang again, and this time his song was even more joyous than at first.

Then the King sent out messengers, to invite all his subjects to the marriage of Robin Redbreast and Jenny Wren. They came from the four corners of the kingdom. Prince and pauper, farmer, blacksmith and learned clerk; and everyone who came was made welcome.

The King made a great feast, and there in the palace the marriage took place. After the ceremony, the King and the Queen led the grand march and everyone danced.

Robin Redbreast was so happy that he flew to the windowsill and sang his joyous song again. Then Young Robin Redbreast and Little Jenny Wren spread their wings and flew away to the brier bush, at the side of the river. And there they have made their home ever since.

THE LITTLE ENGINE THAT COULD
Trade Mark

Chug, chug, chug. Puff, puff, puff. Ding-dong, ding-dong. The little train rumbled over the tracks. She was a happy little train for she had such a jolly load to carry. Her cars were filled full of good things for boys and girls.

There were toy animals—giraffes with long necks, Teddy bears with almost no necks at all, and even a baby elephant. Then there were dolls—dolls with blue eyes and yellow curls, dolls with brown eyes and brown bobbed heads, and the gayest little toy clown you ever saw. And there were cars full of toy engines, aeroplanes, tops, jack-knives, picture puzzles, books, and every kind of thing boys or girls could want.

But that was not all. Some of the cars were filled with all sorts of good things for boys and girls to eat—big golden oranges, red-cheeked apples, bottles of creamy milk for their breakfasts, fresh spinach for their dinners, peppermint drops, and lollypops for after-meal treats.

The little train was carrying all these good things to the good little boys and girls on the other side of the mountain. She puffed

along happily. Then all of a sudden she stopped with a jerk. She simply could not go another inch. She tried and she tried, but her wheels would not turn.

What were all those good little boys and girls on the other side of the mountain going to do without the jolly toys to play with and the wholesome food to eat?

"Here comes a shiny new engine," said the little clown who had jumped out of the train. "Let us ask him to help us."

So all the dolls and toys cried out together:

"Please, Shiny New Engine, do carry our train over the mountain. Our engine has broken down, and the boys and girls on the other side will have no toys to play with and no wholesome food to eat unless you help us."

But the Shiny New Engine snorted: "I pull you? I am a Passenger Engine. I have just carried a fine big train over the mountain, with more cars than you ever dreamed of. My train had sleeping cars, with comfortable berths; a dining-car where waiters bring whatever hungry people want to eat; and parlor cars in which people sit in soft arm-chairs and look out of big plate-glass windows. I carry the likes of you? Indeed not!" And off he steamed to the roundhouse, where engines live when they are not busy.

How sad the little train and all the dolls and toys felt!

Then the little clown called out, "The Passenger Engine is not the only one in the world. Here is another coming, a fine big strong one. Let us ask him to help us."

The little toy clown waved his flag and the big strong engine came to a stop.

"Please, oh, please, Big Engine," cried all the dolls and toys together. "Do pull our train over the mountain. Our engine has broken down, and the good little boys and girls on the other side will have no toys to play with and no wholesome food to eat unless you help us."

But the Big Strong Engine bellowed: "I am a Freight Engine. I have just pulled a big train loaded with costly machines over the mountain. These machines print books and newspapers for grown-ups to read. I am a very important engine indeed. I won't carry the likes of you!" And the Freight Engine puffed off indignantly to the round-house.

The little train and all the dolls and toys were very sad.

"Cheer up," cried the little toy clown. "The Freight Engine is not the only one in the world. Here comes another. He looks very old and tired, but our train is so little, perhaps he can help us."

So the little toy clown waved his flag and the dingy, rusty old engine stopped.

"Please, Kind Engine," cried all the dolls and toys together. "Do pull our train over the mountain. Our engine has broken down, and the boys and girls on the other side will have no toys to play with and no wholesome food to eat unless you help us."

But the rusty old engine sighed: "I am so tired. I must rest my weary wheels. I cannot pull even so little a train as yours over the mountain. I can not. I can not. I can not."

And off he rumbled to the round-house chugging, "I can not. I can not. I can not."

Then indeed the little train was very, very sad, and the dolls and toys were ready to cry.

But the little clown called out, "Here is another engine coming, a little blue engine, a very little one, but perhaps she will help us."

The very little engine came chug, chugging merrily along. When she saw the toy clown's flag, she stopped quickly.

"What is the matter, my friends?" she asked kindly.

"Oh, Little Blue Engine," cried the dolls and toys. "Will you pull us over the mountain? Our engine has broken down and the good boys and girls on the other side will have no toys to play with and no wholesome food to eat, unless you help us. Please, please, help us, Little Blue Engine."

"I'm not very big," said the Little Blue Engine. "They use me only for switching in the yard. I have never been over the mountain."

"But we must get over the mountain before the children awake," said all the dolls and the toys.

The very little engine looked up and saw the tears in the doll's eyes. And she thought of the good little boys and girls on the other side of the mountain who would have no toys and no wholesome food unless she helped.

Then she said, "I think I can. I think I can. I think I can." And she hitched herself to the little train.

She tugged and pulled and pulled and tugged and slowly, slowly, slowly they started off.

The toy clown jumped aboard and all the dolls and the toy animals began to smile and cheer.

Puff, puff, chug, chug, went the little blue engine. "I think I can—I think I can—I think I can—I think I can—I think I can—I think I can—I think I can—I think I can—I think I can."

Up, up, up. Faster and faster and faster and faster the little engine climbed until at last they reached the top of the mountain.

Down in the valley lay the city.

"Hurrah, hurrah," cried the gay little clown and all the dolls and toys. "The good little boys and girls in the city will be happy because you helped us, kind Little Blue Engine."

And the Little Blue Engine smiled and seemed to say as she puffed steadily down the mountain. "I thought I could. I thought I could. I thought I could. I thought I could.

I thought I could.

I thought I could."

THE LION AND THE MOUSE

One evening long, long ago a Lion was asleep in the forest. A party of mice, who lived in the forest saw the King of Beasts sleeping.

"What a huge animal he is!" exclaimed the youngest mouse, whose name was Fuzzytail.

"Yes," said his brother, Grayskin. "And it is only because he is asleep that we dare to be near him."

"Even when he is asleep, I am afraid of him," said another mouse. "Suppose he should wake up!"

"No danger," said Fuzzytail. "He is sound asleep and will sleep until the sun rises."

"I wouldn't be too sure," said Grayskin. "It is said that all cats sleep with one eye open."

"Well, you see this big cat has both of his shut," argued Fuzzytail. "I am going to jump on him."

"Be careful how you run over him. So long as you play on his back and sides, his fur will keep him from feeling your feet; but keep away from his nose, it is very sensitive," warned Grayskin.

"Eek—Eek!" laughed Fuzzytail. "Watch me run right over his nose."

With a sudden movement the King of the Beasts opened his eyes and shook his head. All the mice scampered away as fast as they could. But poor little Fuzzytail was right on his nose, and, before he could escape, the Lion stretched out one great paw and caught him.

"Gr-rr-rr!" growled the Lion.

"Oh, great King of Beasts," begged the trembling little mouse, "please let me go."

"Gr-rr-rr!" the Lion growled again. "Why should I? Haven't you been told that it is dangerous to rouse a sleeping lion? With my paw I can crush you, you silly little animal."

"Oh, please don't," begged Fuzzytail again. "I didn't mean to wake you, and I'll never do it again."

"Well," said the Lion, "I see that you are very young, so I will spare you this time." And, lifting his huge paw, he allowed the trembling little mouse to run into the forest.

After that Fuzzytail and his friends played far away from the sleeping lion. But one evening, as they came out of the forest, he was not asleep as usual. He was rolling around and roaring so that the whole forest echoed.

"What is he roaring at?" they asked one another.

"I am going to see," said Fuzzytail. The others begged him not to go, but the little mouse was determined.

"He set me free when he could have crushed me," he said. "Now he is in trouble and I'm going to help him if I can."

As he came close, he saw the King of Beasts, tangled up in the meshes of a net that hunters had spread for him. The more he roared and rolled about, the more entangled he became.

Suddenly he heard a little voice close to his ear. He stopped his roaring and listened. The voice came again.

"I am the mouse you freed," it said. "If you will just lie still, I will gnaw the ropes that hold you."

The huge Lion lay still and Fuzzytail gnawed at one rope after another with his sharp little teeth. At length the meshes of the net fell away, and the Lion sprang to his feet.

"Thank you, little brother," he said. "I did not know that my deed of kindness would bring me such a rich reward."